ZOO

With thanks to Joseph for his invaluable contribution
—A.B.

Copyright © 1992 by Anthony Browne
All rights reserved
Distributed in Canada by Douglas & McIntyre Ltd.
Library of Congress Control Number: 2001099481
Printed in Hong Kong
First published in Great Britain by Julia MacRae Books, 1992
First American edition published by Alfred A. Knopf, Inc., 1992
Sunburst edition, 2002
1 3 5 7 9 10 8 6 4 2

ZOO

A Sunburst Book • Farrar, Straus and Giroux

My Family

Me.

My brother.

Dad.

Mom.

Last Sunday we all went to the zoo.
Me and my brother were really excited.

But there were masses of cars on the road, and it took ages to get there. After a while Harry and I got really bored. So we had a fight. Harry started crying and Dad told me off. It's not fair, he never tells Harry off. It's always *my* fault.

"What kind of jam do you get stuck in?" asked Dad.

"Don't know," said Harry.

"A traffic jam!" roared Dad.

Everyone laughed except Mom and Harry and me.

When we finally got there Dad *had* to have a quarrel with the man in the ticket booth. He tried to say that Harry was only four and should get in for half-price. (He's five and a half, actually.)

"Highway robbery!" Dad snarled.

Sometimes he can be really embarrassing.

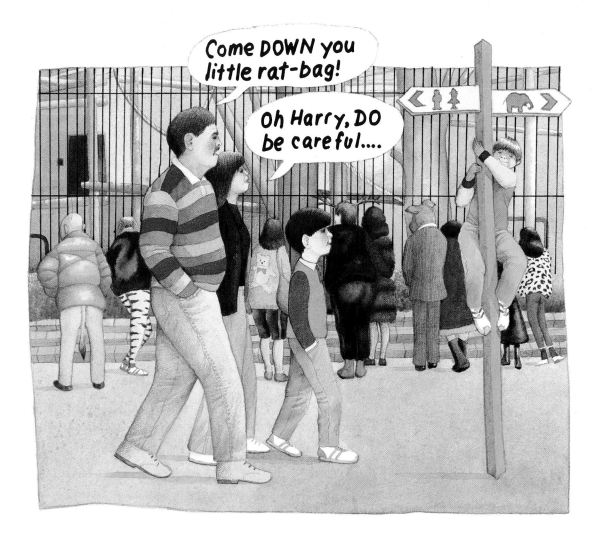

We hadn't gotten a map of the zoo, so we just
wandered around. Me and my brother wanted to
see the gorillas and monkeys, but we had to see
all these boring animals first. We went into the
elephant house, which was really smelly. The
elephant just stood in a corner stuffing its face.

Mom had brought some chocolate, and
Harry and I were hungry.

"Can we have it now?" I asked.

"No, not yet," said Dad.

"Why not?" whined Harry.

"Because," said Dad.

"Because why?" I asked.

"Because I say so," said Dad. It seemed he
was in one of his moods.

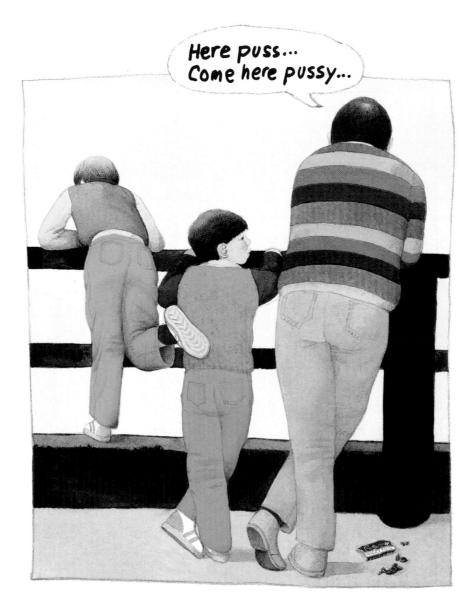

Then we saw the tigers. One of them was just walking along a wall of the cage, then turning around and walking all the way back. Then it would start again.

"Poor thing," said Mom.

"You wouldn't say that if it was chasing after you," snorted Dad. "Look at those nasty teeth!"

Harry and I were starving.

"Can't we have lunch now?" I asked.

"But we just got here," said Mom.

It seemed like we'd been there for hours.
My brother thumped me, so I kicked him,
and we wrestled for a bit, then Dad told
me off.

We looked at the penguins next. I usually
find penguins funny when I see them on TV,
but all I could think of was food.

"What animal can you eat at the zoo?"
asked Dad.

"Don't know," I groaned.

"A hot dog!" howled Dad. He was holding
his stomach and laughing so much that tears
were rolling down his face.

"Come on, boys," said Mom. "Let's get
something to eat."

The café was great. I had a burger and fries and baked beans and loads of ketchup, and chocolate ice cream with raspberry sauce. It was great.

After that we went into the gift shop to spend our pocket money. We each bought a funny monkey hat. "Which one is the monkey?" jeered you-know-who.

Then we had to go and see the polar bear. It looked really stupid, just walking up and down, up and down.

Next we saw the baboons, and they were a bit more interesting. Two of them had a fight.

"They remind me of someone," said Mom. "I can't think who."

The orangutan crouched in a corner and didn't move.
We tried shouting at it and banging on the glass, but it
just ignored us. Miserable thing.

Finally we found the gorillas. They were quite good. Of course Dad had to do his King Kong impersonation, but luckily we were the only ones there.

Then it was time to go home. In the car Mom asked us what was the best part of the day. I said the burger and fries and beans, and Harry said the monkey hats.

Dad said the best part was going home, and asked her what was for dinner.

"I don't think the zoo really is for animals," said Mom. "I think it's for people."

That night I had a very strange dream.

Do you think animals have dreams?